THE CASE OF THE
Vanishing
Caterpillar

ERIC HOGAN & TARA HUNGERFORD

FIREFLY BOOKS

FOR WILFRED & PARIS,
THE ORIGINAL GUMBOOT KIDS.

A FIREFLY BOOK

Published Under License by Firefly Books Ltd. 2019
Copyright © 2019 Gumboot Kids Media Inc.
Book adaptation and realization © 2019 Firefly Books Ltd.
Photographs © Gumboot Kids Media Inc. unless otherwise
specified on page 32.

This book is based on the popular children's shows *Scout &
the Gumboot Kids*, *Daisy & the Gumboot Kids* and *Jessie &
the Gumboot Kids*.

'GUMBOOT KIDS' is a trademark of Gumboot Kids Media Inc., and
an application for registration is pending in Canada. Trademarks
of Gumboot Kids Media Inc. may not be used without express
permission.

First printing

Library of Congress Control Number: 2019930758

Library and Archives Canada Cataloguing in Publication:
Title: The case of the vanishing caterpillar / Eric Hogan & Tara
Hungerford.
Other titles: Scout & the Gumboot Kids (Television program)
Names: Hogan, Eric, 1979- author. | Hungerford, Tara, 1975-
author. | Imagine Create Media, issuing body.
Description: Series statement: A Gumboot Kids nature mystery |
Based on the TV series: Scout & the Gumboot Kids.
Identifiers: Canadiana 20190058307 | ISBN 9780228101932
(hardcover) | ISBN 9780228101949 (softcover)
Subjects: LCSH: Caterpillars—Juvenile literature. | LCSH: Butter-
flies—Life cycles—Juvenile literature. | LCSH: Metamorphosis—
Juvenile literature.
Classification: LCC QL544.2 .H64 2019 | DDC j595.78/9—dc23

Published in the United States by
Firefly Books (U.S.) Inc.
P.O. Box 1338, Ellicott Station
Buffalo, New York 14205

Published in Canada by
Firefly Books Ltd.
50 Staples Avenue, Unit 1
Richmond Hill, Ontario L4B 0A7

Printed in Canada

Canada We acknowledge the financial support of the
Government of Canada.

Scout loves being in his garden, growing flowers and veggies and getting his hands dirty. Today, while digging, he realizes that he hasn't seen his caterpillar friend in a few days.

"Hmm. I wonder where she went?" says Scout. "Perhaps my friend Daisy can help me solve this mystery."

Later that day, Daisy visits for tea.

"What's new, Scout?" asks Daisy.

"Well, something mysterious happened in my garden," replies Scout.

"Oh really? Tell me everything!" says Daisy.

"Here, take a look. I sketched a few observations," says Scout, opening his field notes. "This is a drawing of my caterpillar friend."

"Lovely! I'd like to meet her," remarks Daisy.

"Well I'm afraid you can't," says Scout. "She vanished!"

Caterpillar

"This sounds like a nature mystery!" exclaims Daisy.

"Indeed," agrees Scout. "The Case of the Vanishing Caterpillar."

"I'm so excited," says Daisy. "Let's look for some clues."

"My caterpillar friend liked to hang out on tree branches," notes Scout.

"Look over here," says Daisy. "The leaves on this branch look like they've been nibbled."

"Yes, she loved snacking on leaves," says Scout. "She must have been here recently."

Branch

"Look, Daisy," says Scout. "I sketched another observation in my field notes. This was hanging from the branch this morning, but I don't know what it is. Do you?"

Daisy pulls back the leaves to get a closer look at the branch. "I can see it," says Daisy. "But it looks empty."

"You're right. I wonder what was inside," reflects Scout.

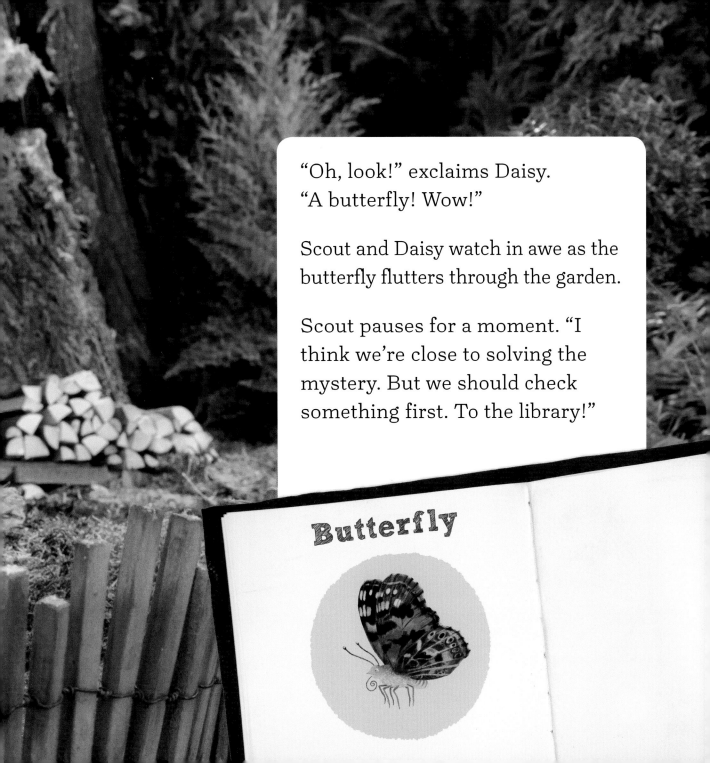

"Oh, look!" exclaims Daisy.
"A butterfly! Wow!"

Scout and Daisy watch in awe as the butterfly flutters through the garden.

Scout pauses for a moment. "I think we're close to solving the mystery. But we should check something first. To the library!"

Butterfly

Scout digs through the books in his library and finds one about butterflies.

"Look!" begins Daisy. "The thing we observed hanging from the branch is called a chrysalis."

"But the chrysalis in my garden was empty... so what was inside?" asks Scout.

"Let's put the clues together to solve The Case of the Vanishing Caterpillar," says Daisy. "We found the branch, an empty chrysalis and a butterfly..."

"I know why the caterpillar vanished!" exclaims Scout. "She turned into a butterfly. Look, here in the book."

Daisy reads aloud:

Fully grown caterpillars attach themselves to a branch before shedding their outside layer of skin to reveal a layer of hard skin underneath called a chrysalis. Inside the chrysalis, the caterpillar grows wings. This is part of a process called metamorphosis. After a few days a butterfly comes out of the chrysalis and flies away. The example shown here is part of the life cycle of a monarch butterfly.

THE LIFE CYCLE OF A BUTTERFLY

Back in the garden, Scout and Daisy celebrate.

"Another case closed!" announces Daisy.

"I can't believe a caterpillar can form a chrysalis and then change itself into a butterfly," says Scout. "Isn't nature marvelous?"

"It sure is," agrees Daisy.

"Now let's pause and have a mindful moment," says Scout. "Things are changing all the time in nature — plants grow, the weather changes and caterpillars turn into butterflies."

Daisy continues, "Metamorphosis shows us that change can be beautiful and graceful. Even you and I change every day. We grow older, taller and learn new things. For instance, today we learned a lot about caterpillars."

"And butterflies," adds Scout.

Later that night, Scout is snuggled in his bed. "When I'm under the covers, I feel like a caterpillar all curled up in a cozy chrysalis. I wonder if tomorrow I'll have wings... Goodnight, Gumboot Kids."

Field Notes

Antennae: The organs on a butterfly's head that allow it to find food, migrate, mate and sleep.

Thorax: The central part of a butterfly's body that contains the muscles that make the legs and wings move.

Abdomen: The central part of a butterfly's body, below the thorax, that contains a tube-like heart, reproductive organs, many breathing spores (spiracles) and most of the digestive system.

Legs: A butterfly has six legs with taste sensors in its feet.

Wings: A butterfly has four wings — two forewings and two hindwings.

A Painted Lady Butterfly

Antennae

Wings

Thorax

Legs

Abdomen

28

Scientists estimate that there are between 15,000 and 20,000 different species of butterfly.

Butterflies often have brightly colored wings with unique patterns made up of tiny scales.

Most butterflies feed on nectar from flowers.

A chrysalis is a hard shell created by a caterpillar in which its transformation takes place.

A butterfly's life cycle, called metamorphosis, is made up of four parts: egg, larva (caterpillar), pupa (chrysalis), and adult (butterfly).

Monarch butterflies are known for their long migration. Every fall, monarch butterflies travel thousands of miles from cold northern climates to warmer climates in Mexico.

Nature Craft

Scout and Daisy were so inspired by solving The Case of the Vanishing Caterpillar that they made a butterfly out of flower petals and leaves. Would you like to make a flower petal butterfly?

STEP 1

Head outside and collect some flower petals and leaves. This craft works best if the flowers are pressed. Place your flowers and leaves flat between two sheets of paper and two heavy books. Leave them for a few days until they're dried and pressed.

STEP 2

Gather some paper and glue. Imagine what you want your butterfly to look like.

STEP 3

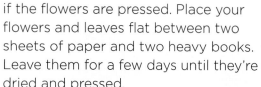

On a sheet of paper, arrange your flower petals and leaves into the butterfly's wings, abdomen and antennae. Glue them to the paper. You can add details with paint, markers or crayons. There is no right or wrong way to make a nature craft, so have fun!

TELEVISION SERIES CREDITS

Created by Eric Hogan and Tara Hungerford
Produced by Tracey Mack
Developed for television with Cathy Moss
Music by Jessie Farrell

Television Consultants

Mindfulness: Molly Stewart Lawlor, Ph.D
Zoology: Michelle Tseng, Ph.D
Botany: Loren Rieseberg, Ph.D

BOOK CREDITS

Based on scripts for television by Tara Hungerford,
Cathy Moss and Eric Hogan
Production Design: Eric Hogan and Tara Hungerford
Head of Production: Tracey Mack
Character Animation: Deanna Partridge-David
Graphic Design: Rio Trenaman, Gurjant Singh
Sekhon and Lucas Green
Photography: Sean Cox
Illustration: Kate Jeong

Special thanks to the Gumboot Kids cast and crew,
CBC Kids, Shaw Rocket Fund, Independent Media
Fund, The Bell Fund, Canada Media Fund, Creative
BC, Playology, and our friends and family.

ADDITIONAL PHOTO CREDITS

30 Anick Violette (flower petal butterfly craft)

Shutterstock.com
16 Super Prin; 20 Brek P. Kent (caterpillar);
20–21 FWStudio (green background), Geza Farkas
(metamorphosis); 30 Megapixels (glue), Svrid79
(flower petals)

More GUMBOOT KIDS Nature Mysteries

Visit Scout and Daisy
gumbootkids.com

THE CASE OF THE
Story Rock
A GUMBOOT KIDS Nature Mystery

THE CASE OF THE
Growing Bird Feeder
A GUMBOOT KIDS Nature Mystery

THE CASE OF THE
Wooden Timekeeper
A GUMBOOT KIDS Nature Mystery